Dhansee & Randy

K Abirami

Ukiyoto Publishing

All global publishing rights are held by

Ukiyoto Publishing

Published in 2023

Content Copyright © K Abirami

ISBN 9789360162443

All rights reserved.

No part of this publication may be reproduced, transmitted, or stored in a retrieval system, in any form by any means, electronic, mechanical, photocopying, recording or otherwise, without the prior permission of the publisher.

The moral rights of the author have been asserted.

This is a work of fiction. Names, characters, businesses, places, events, locales, and incidents are either the products of the author's imagination or used in a fictitious manner. Any resemblance to actual persons, living or dead, or actual events is purely coincidental.

This book is sold subject to the condition that it shall not by way of trade or otherwise, be lent, resold, hired out or otherwise circulated, without the publisher's prior consent, in any form of binding or cover other than that in which it is published.

*This title is produced in Association with
Pachyderm Tales*

www.pachydermtales.com

ACKNOWLEDGEMENT

I whole heartedly thank,

    Mohanasundari Jaganathan,

(Managing Director of Sharp Electrodes Pvt Ltd)

for funding this project.

Without her, this book would not be possible!

This book was a part of workshop conducted in our college, NGM College Pollachi and Pachyderm Tales.

I whole heartedly thank our management, our teachers and HOD of English Dept, NGM as well as Suja Mam for this initiative.

Thanks to my friend to support and help me to complete my work.

For a child, after their parents, the most **precious** thing to them is their toys.

Every child has their own **favourite** toy and a story behind it.

Here comes the sweet

little girl of our story,

The **Princess** of their

home, Dhansee!

With her **favourite**

toy, Randy.

(A golden-brown dog)

Dhansee & Randy   5

Dhansee always carried Randy with her to **everywhere**.

Randy is her lucky toy; she always considers herself to be **lucky** because of Randy and she has a good reason to feel such way.

Dhansee & Randy 7

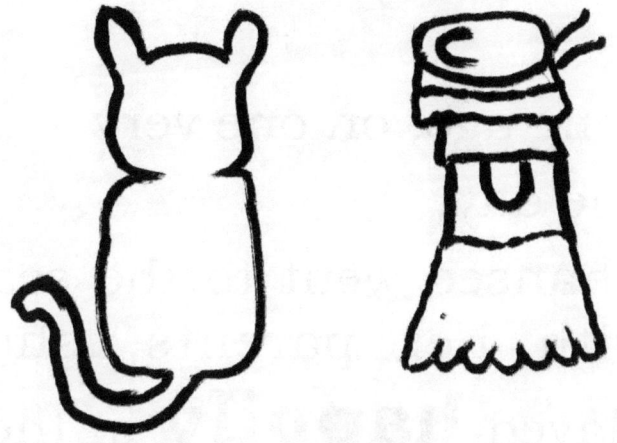

Long ago, on one very fine day,

Dhansee went to the sea with her parents, she played **happily** in the waves.

Her sole **concentration** was in playing with the waves.

She was so **immersed** in her **happiness** that she actually lost the sight of her parents.

When she noticed that she was alone, she started crying and **searched** for her parents in the **crowd** and all around the **shore.**

But, for more than an hour she could not find them.

Our Little Dhansee stared crying **harder** and walked around on the shore **pointlessly** in the hope of finding them.

After some time, she had noticed her toy – Randy; **lying** on the shore. She ran towards the toy to take it and cried aloud while holding it.

Then, suddenly she felt someone touching her shoulder, and that was her mother...

Dhansee & Randy

Dhansee **hugged** her mother and sobbed so hard. Then, her mother gently **advised** Dhansee to always be careful of her **surroundings** and follow her parents no matter what happens.

Dhansee, with her face all red because of crying agreed with her mother saying "yes mom".

After that incident Randy became Dhansee's **favourite** toy.

Dhansee & Randy

According

to her, she found her **parents** only because of the toy – Randy.

Then the toy Randy became the biggest part of her childhood.

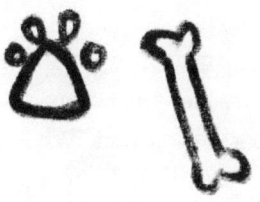

The Author

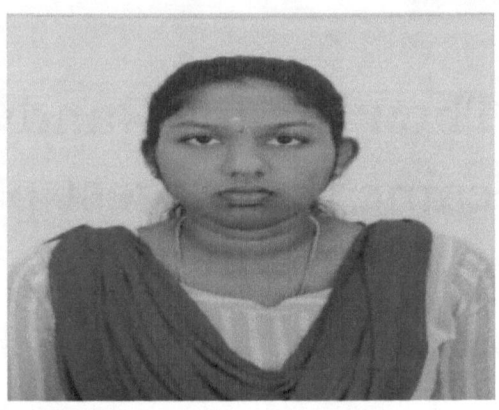

K. Abirami, a final year graduate of English Literature, studying at NGM college. She is a budding writer who intends to write for children and entertain them in the best way possible. Dhansee and Randy is her first book where she had put in her creativity in children's storytelling. She foresees herself as a person who mingles and interacts with a lot more children and learn about their interests.

www.ingramcontent.com/pod-product-compliance
Lightning Source LLC
LaVergne TN
LVHW041643070526
838199LV00053B/3542